I WAS SO MAD

BY MERCER MAYER

SCHOLASTIC INC.

New York Toronto London Auckland Sydney
Mexico City New Delhi Hong Kong Buenos Aires

ISBN 0-439-77811-5

20 19 18 17 16 15 14   8 9 10/0

Printed in the U.S.A.   23

First Scholastic printing, March 2005

I wanted to keep some frogs in the bathtub but Mom wouldn't let me.

I was so mad.

I wanted to play
with my little sister's
dollhouse but Dad
wouldn't let me.

I was so mad.

I wanted to play
hide-and-seek in
the clean sheets
but Grandma said,
"No, you can't."

I was just so mad.

I wanted to water the garden
but Grandpa said,
"No, you can't."

So I decided to
decorate the house
but Grandpa said,
"No, you can't do
that, either."

Was I ever mad.

Dad said, "Why don't you play in the sandbox?"

I didn't want to do that.

Mom said, "Why don't you play on the slide?"

I didn't want to do that, either.
I was too mad.

I wanted to practice my juggling show, instead.

But Mom said, "No, you can't."

I wanted to tickle the goldfish but Mom said, "Leave the goldfish alone."

"You won't let me do anything
I want to do," I said.
"I guess I'll run away."

That's how mad I was.

So I packed my wagon
with my favorite toys.

And I packed a bag of cookies
to eat on the way.

Then I walked out the front door.
But my friends were going to the
park to play ball.
"Can you come, too?" they asked.

And Mom said I could.

I'll run away tomorrow if I'm still so mad.